Space, Time, Rhythm and Rhyme

Russell Stannard was formerly Professor of Physics at the Open University in Milton Keynes. He has travelled widely in Europe and the United States of America, researching high energy nuclear physics. He was recently awarded an OBE for services to physics and the popularization of science.

Space, Time, Rhythm and Rhyme

RUSSELL STANNARD

illustrated by John Levers

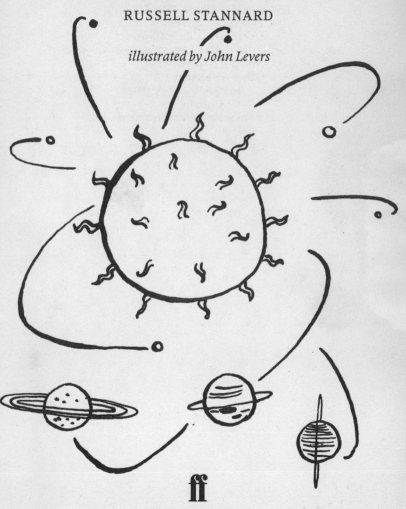

ff

faber and faber

First published in 1999
by Faber and Faber Limited
3 Queen Square London WC1N 3AU

Typeset by Faber and Faber Ltd
Printed in England by Mackays of Chatham plc, Chatham, Kent

A CIP record for this book
is available from the British Library

ISBN 0–571–19579–2

2 4 6 8 10 9 7 5 3 1

Contents

Introduction

The Universe! What could be more awesome and wonderful? And yet, to hear some scientists talk, you would think it was really boring. Why?

It's a bit like chocolate. Eat a bar of chocolate and it's scrummy. Work in a chocolate factory, where you can eat as much as you like, all day long, every day, and it no longer seems all that special.

Same with the Universe. When you first learn about it, it's mindboggling. But if you're a busy scientist investigating the Universe day in, day out, there comes a point where you stop being boggled. You have lots of sums to do, and formulae to work out, and stuff like that. We scientists enjoy that sort of thing – but not everybody does. We talk our own scientific language, using big words. We tend to forget that nobody else has a clue what we're on about. No wonder we send people to sleep.

But I have a plan. I am going to tell you about the Universe, but it won't just be me. To make it more interesting, I shall bring some *poets* along with us. Poets are good at capturing a sense of wonder and of fun. They make you think; they make you laugh. Serious poets, funny poets, young poets – they are all coming along with us as we set off for outer space!

When I Heard the Learn'd Astronomer

When I heard the learn'd astronomer
When the proofs, the figures, were ranged in columns
   before me,
When I was shown the charts and diagrams, to add,
   divide, and measure them,
When I sitting heard the astronomer where he lectured
   with much applause in the lecture-room,
How soon unaccountable I became tired and sick,
Till rising and gliding out I wander'd off by myself,
In the mystical moist night-air, and from time to time,
Look'd up in perfect silence at the stars.

Walt Whitman

Space, Time, Rhythm and Rhyme

The Sky Above

When I was a little boy I used to think the night sky was a great hollow dome with twinkly lights stuck to it. I first got this idea one Saturday morning. My mother had taken my brother and me to a cinema in Brixton, London. It had a ceiling just like that – a dome painted dark blue, with little white lights scattered all over it to look like stars. In fact, long, long ago, it wasn't just children who thought that way; everyone thought the sky covered the Earth like a dome.

Rain

There are holes in the sky
Where the rain gets in,
But they're ever so small
That's why rain is thin.

Spike Milligan

One night I sneaked out of the house with my dad's powerful torch – without him knowing. The idea was to shine it on to the sky. That way I would see its reflection on the underside of the dome. The brightness of the reflected light would then give me an idea as to how far away the dome was. The fainter the patch, the higher the dome must be.

And what did I find? Nothing! No matter how hard I peered up at the sky, I couldn't see the patch of light at all. I

3

decided that the sky must be much, much higher than I had thought. It must be way, way above the chimney tops.

Come to think of it, that was my very first scientific experiment. A measurement of the size of the Universe! (And I even managed to smuggle the torch back into the house without Dad knowing I had 'borrowed' it.)

I Remember, I Remember

I remember, I remember,
The fir trees dark and high.
I used to think their slender tops
Were close against the sky.
It was a childish ignorance.
But now 'tis little joy
To know I'm farther off from Heaven
Than when I was a boy.

Thomas Hood

These days, of course, everybody knows there is no hollow dome up there. The sky just goes on and on – possibly for ever.

I sometimes get to thinking of that torch beam. It is some sixty years since I first sent it off on its journey into space. So far, it has travelled 550 million million kilometres!

Our Home, the Earth

Before telling you what else is out there (apart from my torch beam), let me first mention one or two things about the Earth.

A second idea I had when I was small was that the Earth was flat. Well, why not? It *looks* flat – more or less. But doesn't that mean you get into trouble when you get to the edge? Apart from the danger of falling off, won't all the water drain out of the seas and over the edge? No wonder sailors used to get worried about travelling too far from home.

Nowadays we know that the Earth is not flat at all; it is shaped like a gigantic ball. There is no edge. Travel far enough over its surface and you land back where you started.

I Saw a Man Pursuing the Horizon

I saw a man pursuing the horizon;
Round and round they sped.
I was disturbed at this;
I accosted the man.
'It is futile,' I said,
'You can never –'
'You lie,' he cried,
And ran on.

Stephen Crane

But what about the poor Australians? There might not be an edge to fall over, but those living on the opposite side of the 'ball' will be *underneath*. Doesn't that mean they have to hang on for dear life to stop themselves falling off the Earth? Are all the loose things in Australia nailed down (er, nailed *up*)?

Australia

Quite obviously in Australia
Everything's upside down;
And you must be an absolute failure
If you happen to wear a crown.

Do you walk, to get through a door,
On the ceiling? Does a bird
Perch out of harm on the floor?
Is 'top' a rather rude word?

Is headball played and elevennis?
If you hate anyone is it love?
Of course, they don't know where heaven is
Except that it's not up above.

Are holidays longer than terms?
Are humbugs good for you?
No doubt deep in the sky are worms,
And served first is last in the queue.

Do dogs sniff each other's noses
And wag them when they are glad?
Are dandelions not roses
Carefully grown by Dad?

6

Do children go to the office?
Does Mother tell awful lies?
And Grandpa buy comics and toffees,
Gran's skirt give her chilly thighs?

If so, I'll not go to Australia,
Where at jokes a listener sobs.
Besides, I prefer a dahlia
To grow flowers rather than knobs.

Roy Fuller

It's all right; we don't have to worry about our Australian friends. The important thing is that there is no special 'down' direction. It is not that things fall *down*; rather, they fall *towards each other*. An apple falling off a tree falls towards the centre of the Earth. And that is true of all apples, wherever their tree happens to be on the Earth's globe – including Australian apples. And that's why loose things lie on the ground all round the Earth; they are all trying to get to the centre of the Earth, until something – the ground – gets in the way.

It's all due to gravity . . .

Isaac Newton

Sir Isaac Newton sure was smart,
beneath the apple tree.
When one fell off and hit his head,
he said, 'Wow, gravity!'

For Newton was a genius
and not a common slouch.

A genius cries 'Gravity!'
Most others just say 'ouch!'

Calvin Miller

With everything pulling on everything else with the force of gravity, they all try to get as close together as they possibly can. That's why the Earth ends up round. Being round is the best way of packing things together tightly.

And what's good for the Earth is good for most things in space. That's why we find the Sun, the Moon and the stars are all round.

So much for the shape of the Earth. The next question is: What does the Earth *do*?

For a start, it doesn't stay still; it spins. The Earth is like a top; it spins about an imaginary line drawn through the North Pole, passing through the centre of the Earth, and coming out at the South Pole.

The Spinning Earth

The earth, they say,
spins round and round.
It doesn't look it
from the ground,
and never makes
a spinning sound.

And water never
swirls and swishes
from oceans full

of dizzy fishes,
and shelves don't lose
their pans and dishes.

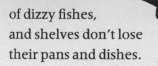

And houses don't go whirling by,
or puppies swirl around the sky,
or robins spin instead of fly.

It may be true
what people say
about one spinning
night and day . . .
but I keep wondering, anyway.

Aileen Fisher

The reason we don't get dizzy, and are not flung off into space, is that the Earth spins quite slowly. It takes one day to do a complete turn. In fact, that is what we *mean* by a 'day'; a day is the time it takes to go from the Sun being directly overhead (noon), through the afternoon, evening, night, and following morning, until the Sun is directly overhead again (noon next day).

A New Hymn to the Sun

Sun,
what did you do
with the dark?
chase her away?
do her in
and devour her?

Or did you embrace
and hide her away
in your arms of light?

Is the dark your enemy,
something you eat?
or love maybe:
did she get so dark
not knowing where you were
all night?

And when you arrived,
did she lose herself
in you, your light?

Maybe your brother
and sister,
and your mother
asked you both
to take turns
watching over the world.

Don't you die,
are you immortals?
I praise you both,

and especially you,
O Sun.

Subramanya Bharati

It is not the Sun going round us, rising in the east and going down in the west (although it *looks* that way). The Sun stays where it is. It is we who are spinning – first turning one side of the Earth towards the Sun (daytime), then turning to face away from it (night-time), before turning to face it once more, and so on.

Because of the Earth's spinning motion, our life dances to a particular rhythm – working and playing during the day, sleeping and dreaming at night.

All Things Pass

All things pass
A sunrise does not last all morning
All things pass
A cloudburst does not last all day

11

All things pass
Nor a sunset all night
All things pass
What always changes?

Earth . . . sky . . . thunder . . .
mountain . . . water . . .
wind . . . fire . . . lake . . .

These change
And if these do not last

Do man's visions last?
Do man's illusions?

Take things as they come

All things pass

Lao-Tzu

Our Space Companion, the Moon

Unlike the Sun, the Moon *does* go round the Earth. It takes a month to make the complete journey. Why does it not go drifting off into space? Well, you know how you can whirl a stone round your head in a circle if you keep pulling on it by a length of string. In much the same way, the Earth's invisible gravity stretches out into space and holds the Moon on its course, as it travels in a circle around us.

The light of the Moon is much gentler than that of the Sun. It can be very beautiful and mysterious. Lovers find it romantic. Even the animals seem to be enchanted by the light of the full Moon.

The Harvest Moon

The flame-red moon, the harvest moon,
Rolls along the hills, gently bouncing,
A vast balloon,
Till it takes off, and sinks upward
To lie in the bottom of the sky, like a gold doubloon.

The harvest moon has come,
Booming softly through heaven, like a bassoon.
And earth replies all night, like a deep drum.

So people can't sleep,
So they go out where elms and oak trees keep

A kneeling vigil, in a religious hush.
The harvest moon has come!

And all the moonlit cows and all the sheep
Stare up at her petrified, while she swells
Filling heaven, as if red hot, and sailing
Closer and closer like the end of the world

Till the gold fields of stiff wheat
Cry 'We are ripe, reap us!' and the rivers
Sweat from the melting hills.

Ted Hughes

Something that has always fascinated people is the way the Moon appears to change shape.

Moon

A white face
in the night.
A ten
pence piece
in the dark
of your pocket
shining
secretly bright.

A cold light
blue-circled
with winter's
frostbite.
A sliver
a shiver of ice.

A melon slice slung
in a sky spiced
with stars.
An ivory horn
still there
with the dawn.

And a great
golden plate
risen with dusk.
Coming to rest
low over fields
heavy
with harvest.

Ann Bonner

In fact there is no mystery about this. It is not that the Moon itself changes shape – it always remains a round ball. It is just that as the Moon travels round the Earth, different parts of its surface turn to face the Sun. Like the Earth, it gives out no light of its own; it can only reflect the light it receives from the Sun. If the Sun is shining on it from the side, then we see only that part of it lit up. When the Moon is positioned so that the Sun shines full on to it, then we get the chance of seeing the whole of the face of the 'man in the Moon'. It takes a month for the Moon to go through its various 'phases' – the time it takes for it to travel round the Earth to its starting point once more.

On certain special nights, when the Moon is full, it gradually darkens – a shadow falls across it. Later that night, the shadow passes, and the Moon brightens up again.

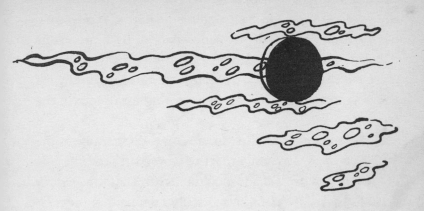

Eclipse of the Moon

Whose shadow's that?

Who walked in the evening
at his own ghost's back?

Who trod in the circle,
left a toe-print on the frozen pond?

Who looked in the mirror
and clouded the glass?

Who snatched the white moth
in his closed fist?

Who drowned
reaching for the coin?

Gillian Clarke

On a sunny day, you cast a shadow. Everything the Sun shines on casts a shadow – including the Earth. As the Moon travels round the Earth it spends part of its time on the opposite side of the Earth to the Sun. When that happens, there is a chance it will pass through the shadow cast by the Earth. And that is what happens during an eclipse of the Moon.

On other occasions, the Moon is on the same side as the Sun. Now there is a chance that the Moon will get in the way of the Sun and cast a shadow on the Earth. That can be *really* alarming – to have the Sun suddenly disappear in the middle of the day! Ancient people got frightened it might not come back. Nowadays, no one worries about such things. Scientists who know how to work out the movements of the Moon and the Earth (they are called astronomers) can tell us in advance when to expect an eclipse of the Sun or the Moon.

The Sun; Source of Life

The Sun looks about the same size as the Moon in the sky. But how big something *looks* depends not only on its size, but also on how far away it is.

How to Reach the Sun . . .
    on a Piece of Paper

Take a sheet of paper
and fold it,
and fold it again,
and again, and again.
By the 6th fold
it is 1 centimetre thick.

By the 11th fold
it will be 32 centimetres thick,
and by the 15th fold
– 5 metres.

At the 20th fold
it measures 160 metres.
At the 24th fold,
– 2. 5 kilometres
and by fold 30
is 160 kilometres high.

At the 35th fold
– 5,000 kilometres.
At the 43rd fold
it will reach to the moon.

And by fold 52
will stretch from here
    to the sun!
Take a sheet of paper.
Go on.
    Try it!

Wes Magee

The Sun is much further from us than the Moon is. So, with it *looking* the same size as the Moon, it must *actually* be much bigger. In fact, one million Earths would fit inside the Sun!

For that reason, it is the Earth that goes round the Sun, not the Sun round the Earth. The Earth is kept in its nearly circular path, or orbit, by the gravity force from the Sun (in the same way as the Moon, remember, was guided along by the Earth's gravity force).

The Earth takes one year to go right round the Sun – that's what we mean by a 'year'.

To the Terrestrial Globe

Roll on, thou ball, roll on!
Through pathless realms of Space
            Roll on!
What though I'm in a sorry case?
What though I cannot meet my bills?
What though I suffer toothache's ills?

What though I swallow countless pills?
Never *you* mind!
Roll on!

Roll on, thou ball, roll on!
Through seas of inky air
Roll on!
It's true I've got no shirts to wear;
It's true my butcher's bill is due;
It's true my prospects all look blue –
But don't let that unsettle you!
Never *you* mind!
Roll on!

W. S. Gilbert

So we have the daily rhythm given by the Earth's spin; the monthly rhythm of the Moon going round the Earth; and now the yearly rhythm of the Earth's journey round the Sun.

Outer space is like a poem. Poems have a certain rhythm to them. They also make repeating patterns of the sounds and the shapes of words on the page. In the same way space has its rhythms; it also has repeating shapes – usually round shapes, and elliptical (nearly circular) orbits.

So we go round the Sun. But what exactly *is* the Sun? It is a huge round ball of fire. It has a temperature measured in *millions* of degrees.

I Can't Take the Sun No More, Man

I can't take the sun no more, Man.
I buy fifty cans of cola,
I take my clothes off,
But I'm still hot.
I might as well take off my skin
It's so so so so hot, Man.
I just can't take the sun no more.
I might as well take myself apart
Before the sun melts me.
It's so so so so so so so so so so
Hot, Man.
Just can't take the sun, Man.

Linval Quinland

Get too close to the Sun and you will be burnt to a cinder. Get too far away from it and you will freeze to death (outer space is very cold). The Earth is at just the right distance from the Sun: not too hot; not too cold. The Sun's gentle warmth makes the crops grow. These give both us and the animals the food we need. Without the Sun, there would be no life.

Sun

Lightbringer
Joymaker
Nightchaser
Cloudshaker.

Foodgrower
Gloomfighter
Heatgiver
Moonlighter.

Sleepender
Icebreaker
Leafrouser
Plantwaker.

Skinbrowner
Nosepeeler
Feetwarmer
Hearthealer.

Steve Turner

We have said how the Earth goes round the Sun. But that doesn't mean the Sun sits still. This great ball of fire also travels silently through the emptiness of space. The Earth keeps it company on its long journeys.

The World

It burns in the void,
Nothing upholds it.
Still it travels.

Travelling the void
Upheld by burning
Nothing is still.

Burning it travels.
The void upholds it.
Still it is nothing.

Nothing it travels
A burning void
Upheld by stillness.

Kathleen Raine

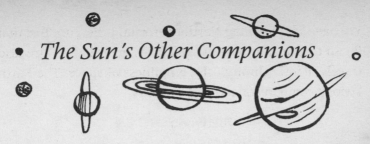

The Sun's Other Companions

Besides the Sun and the Moon, there are the stars – those tiny pinpricks of light. In order to make out what they are, we need help.

Ever used a magnifying glass? Pure magic. A piece of wonky glass (called a *lens*) cunningly shaped to bend the light passing through it in just the right way as to make everything seem bigger! It's like peering into an alien world.

The Magnifying Glass

With this round glass
I can make *Magic* talk –
A myriad shells show
In a scrap of chalk;

Of but an inch of moss
A forest – flowers and trees;
A drop of water
Like a hive of bees.

I lie in wait and watch
How the deft spider jets
The woven web-silk
From his spinnerets;

The tigerish claws he has!
And oh! the silly flies
That stumble into his net –
With all those eyes!

Not even the tiniest thing
But this my glass
Will make more marvellous,
And itself surpass.

Yes, and with lenses like it,
Eyeing the moon,
'Twould seem you'd walk there
In an afternoon!

Walter de la Mare

Not only can lenses make tiny things look big, they can make far-off things seem closer. Lenses and curved mirrors – put them together and we have a telescope.

While most of the starry pinpricks of light remain fixed, making the same patterns of dots night after night, not all do. A few are free to wander about. Through our telescope we can see that these are the other planets. Like the Earth, they go round and round the Sun. There are nine altogether. Closest to the Sun is Mercury; then come Venus, Earth, Mars, Jupiter, Saturn, Uranus, Neptune, and finally Pluto. Together, they and the Sun make up the Solar System.

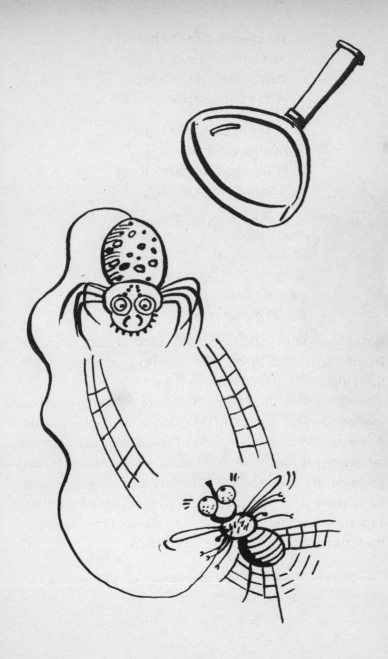

Our Solar System

We made a model of the Solar System
On our school field after lunch.
Sir chose nine of us
To be planets
And he parked the rest of the class
In the middle of the field
In a thoroughly messy bunch.
'You're the sun,' he brays,
'Big, huge; stick your arms out
In all directions
To show the sun's rays.'
The bit about sticking arms out
Really wasn't very wise
And I don't mind telling you
A few fingers and elbows
Got stuck in a few eyes.
Big Bill took a poke at Tony
And only narrowly missed him,
And altogether it looked
More like a shambles
Than the start of the Solar System.
The nine of us who were planets
Didn't get a lot of fun:
I was Mercury and I stood
Like a Charlie
Nearest of all to the sun,
And all the sun crowd
Blew raspberries and shouted,

'This is the one we'll roast!
We're going to scorch you up, Titch,
You'll be like a black slice of toast!'
Katy was Venus and Val was Earth
And Neville Stephens was Mars,
And the sun kids shouted and
Wanted to know
Could he spare them any of his Bars.
A big gap then to Jupiter (Jayne)
And a bigger one still to Saturn
And Sir's excited and rambling on
About the System's mighty pattern.
'Now, a walloping space to Uranus,' he bawls,
It's quite a bike ride away from the sun.'
Ha blooming ha – at least somebody here's
Having a load of fun.
He's got two planet kids left
And Karen's moaning
About having to walk so far:
She's Neptune – I suppose Sir's
Cracking some joke about
Doing X million miles by car.
Pete's Pluto – 'The farthest flung of all,'
Says Sir,
He's put by the hedge and rests,
But soon he starts picking blackberries
And poking at old bird's nests.
'Of course,' yells Sir, 'the scale's not right
But it'll give you
A rough idea.

Now, when I blow my whistle
I want you all to start on your orbits –
Clear?'
Well, it wasn't of course,
And most of the class, well,
Their hearts weren't really in it,
Still, Sir's OK so we gave it a go,
With me popping round the sun
About ten times a minute,
And Pluto on the hedge ambling round
Fit to finish his orbit next year.
We'd still have been there but
A kid came out of the school and yelled,
'The bell's gone and the school bus's here!'
Well, the Solar System
Broke up pretty fast,
And my bus money had gone from my sock
And I had to borrow.
I suppose we'll have to draw diagrams
And write about it tomorrow.

Eric Finney

As well as the planets there are many smaller rocks going round the Sun. Some travel in orbits shaped like squashed circles (called 'ellipses'). This means they come swooping in quite close to the Sun as they go round the tight part of their orbit, before swinging out into distant space once more. When they are in close, they heat up because of the Sun's rays and give off clouds of gas and steam and dust. The cloud streams away like a tail, so big and brightly lit it can often be seen without a telescope. For a few days we are treated to the spectacular sight of a *comet*.

The Comet

Swifter by far than any star that fell
comes the passing stranger;

veiled by the cosmic hand
in shrouds of light,
mystic and pale;

charting its way from somewhere in the night,
beyond the known frontiers.

Like some fair pilgrim bound
to find the shrine,
the source of life;

thundering, silent . . . riding stellar winds,
the traveller forges on.

Its roller-coaster ride
will lead it far
from whence it came,

but one day it will sweep a splendid arc
in the vaulted heavens,

to blaze a mighty trail
that stirs its heart,
and turn for home.

Patti Lynn

Another wonderful sight is that of a falling star. Suddenly, without warning, there appears a streak of light that hurtles across the sky – and is gone.

Stars, I Have Seen Them Fall

Stars, I have seen them fall,
But when they drop and die
No star is lost at all
From all the star-sown sky.
The toil of all that be
Helps not the primal fault;
It rains into the sea,
And still the sea is salt.

A. E. Housman

The reason why there are still the same number of stars in the sky after you have seen one of them fall, is that a falling star is not a real star at all. It's just a tiny speck of dirt that has come hurtling into the Earth's atmosphere from space and got burned up (just like some man-made satellites re-entering the Earth's atmosphere get burned up). Where did the bit of dirt come from? From the tail of an old comet. Each year as the Earth passes through the same region of space where the debris from the tail is, we get falling stars – or, as we prefer to call them, *meteors*. That's why there are particularly good nights to go out looking for them (9–13 August, 14–17 November, and 10–13 December).

The Meteors

The meteors are slipping
Like skaters on the sky!
The meteors are whipping
Their lashes round the sky!
Here another splashes!
There another flashes!
And smashes into ashes
Far from the sky.

Slim silver fishes,
All and each
Are swift sly wishes
Swimming out of reach.
If you will go fishing,
You must do your wishing
Before they finish swishing
And fall on the beach.

The meteors are sliding
All along the sky!
The meteors are gliding
All about the sky!
Shimmering stems of flowers!
Dripping summer showers!
The meteors are riding
All round the sky!

Eleanor Farjeon

Once in a while, a meteor is caused by something bigger than a bit of dirt – it might be a chunk of rock or iron ore. Because it is big, not all of it is burned up in the atmosphere, and a lump of it arrives at the Earth's surface. If it crashes on land, it can make a big crater and cause lots of damage. But don't worry; there's no need to wear a crash helmet to school. Mostly they fall into the oceans or in open country. (It is easier for them to hit an ocean than score a bull's-eye on the top of your head.)

Splat

Some days a hunk of metal
falls from the sky,
usually in the desert
or the deep, green sea.

What's it doing up there?
It's not metal litter
(which wouldn't fly!).
What could it be?

Is it bits of armour
that fell from Heaven,
or chunks of tanks
that exploded high?

Or aeroplanes of aliens
on tourist trips,
till drunken meteors
ploughed on through?

Do bones ever fall,
or the odd weird skull?
What about clothing?
A size fifty shoe?

Do birds get clobbered
as a hunk falls,
or even yachtspeople
miles out to sea?

Not to mention Piccadilly
on a Friday night.
Imagine the splat,
if the hunk wasn't shy.

Matthew Sweeney

The Stars

We have talked about the wandering stars that turned out to be the other planets of our Solar System. We have spoken of falling stars, and said they were not real stars at all – just bits of dirt. It is now time to turn to the *proper* stars.

Shooting Stars

Under cover of daylight they creep up on us
And on cloudy nights close in, slowly but surely

We are surrounded and outnumbered
If it is clear tonight, take a look for yourself

Notice how they keep still while you are watching
Then, as soon as you blink, they have moved

They think you won't notice but you do
The sinister game of statues they are playing

That is why I am out here every night
Rifle in hand, picking them off

Trouble is they are fearless. Kill one
And at the speed of light another takes its place

Aliens with all the time in the world
Licking their lips. Twinkling ever closer.

Roger McGough

There are lots of stars. On clear dark nights it is hard to count them all.

How Many Stars?

When I was a boy
I would ask my dad:
'How many stars are there hanging in the sky?'
'More than enough, son,
More than I could say.
Enough to keep you counting
Till your dying day.'

When I was a boy
I would ask my dad:
'How many fishes are there swimming in the sea?'
'More than enough, son,
More than I could say.
Enough to keep you counting
Till your dying day.'

When I was a boy
I would ask my dad:
'How many creepy-crawlies are there in the world?'
'More than enough, son,
More than I could say.
Enough to keep you counting
Till your dying day.'

It seemed like there wasn't anything my dad didn't know.

Colin McNaughton

There are many more stars than you might think. Most are too faint to be seen with the naked eye. But look through a telescope and it's a different story. Point it at a patch of sky that seems empty, and you find it is not empty at all. There are masses of stars wherever you look. How many altogether? 10,000 million million million!

Who Are You?

'Who are You?'
Says One to Two.
Says Two to One 'I'm plenty'.
'Think again!'
Says little Ten,
And, 'Think again!' says Twenty.

William Brighty Rands

One way to get your mind round the phantasmagorical number of stars, is to take a look at the full stop at the end of this sentence. Small, isn't it? How many would it take to completely cover this page so that none of the white paper could be seen any more? Get a sharp pencil, start from the top left corner, and fill in the whole page with tiny dots no bigger than a full stop. (On second thoughts – DON'T! It would take far too long.)

Now imagine the whole surface of the Earth to be covered with sheets of paper (waterproof paper to float on the wet bits). Suppose all those sheets were completely covered with full stops so that again none of the white paper showed through. Each full stop would stand for one of the stars in the sky. That's how many there are.

Escape at Bedtime

The lights from the parlour and kitchen shone out
Through the blinds and the windows and bars;
And high overhead and all moving about,
There were thousands of millions of stars.
There ne'er were such thousands of leaves on a tree,
Nor of people in church or the Park,
As the crowds of the stars that looked down upon me,
And that glittered and winked in the dark.
The Dog, and the Plough, and the Hunter, and all,
And the star of the sailor, and Mars,
These shone in the sky, and the pail by the wall
Would be half full of water and stars.
They saw me at last, and they chased me with cries,
And they soon had me packed into bed;
But the glory kept shining and bright in my eyes,
And the stars going round in my head.

Robert Louis Stevenson

But what actually *is* a star? Even through a powerful telescope it still looks like a tiny twinkling dot.

The Star

Twinkle, twinkle, little star,
How I wonder what you are!
Up above the world so high,
Like a diamond in the sky.

When the blazing sun is gone,
When he nothing shines upon,
Then you show your little light,
Twinkle, twinkle, all the night.

Then the traveller in the dark,
Thanks you for your tiny spark,
He could not see which way to go,
If you did not twinkle so.

In the dark blue sky you keep,
And often through my curtains peep,
For you never shut your eye,
Till the sun is in the sky.

As your bright and tiny spark,
Lights the traveller in the dark –
Though I know not what you are,
Twinkle, twinkle, little star.

Jane Taylor

We now know that each star is a huge sun – just like our own Sun. The reason they look so tiny is that they are so far away from us. If we were able to travel across space and get up close to one, we would find it was a great ball of fire. It might even have planets going round it, like our own Sun.

Just think of all those solar systems out there.

The Stars

The stars rushed forth tonight
Fast on the faltering light;
So thick those stars did lie
No room was left for sky;
And to my upturned stare
A snowstorm filled the air.

Stars lay like yellow pollen
That from a flower has fallen;
And single stars I saw
Crossing themselves in awe;
Some stars in sudden fear
Fell like a falling tear.

What is the eye of man,
This little star that can
See all those stars at once,
Multitudinous suns,
Making of them a wind
That blows across the mind?

If eye can nothing see
But what is part of me,
I ask and ask again
With a persuasive pain,
What thing, O God, am I,
This mote and mystery?

Andrew Young

How are stars arranged in the sky? Are they just scattered about any old how?

From earliest times, it was thought they were arranged in patterns. These are called 'constellations'. Just as you sometimes imagine a cloud to be in the form of a face or animal, so groups of stars might look like a bear, plough, goat, crab, and so on. Some people believe their lives are controlled by the stars that make up these shapes. They look up their horoscope in newspapers to see 'what the stars say'.

Without wanting to be too much of a spoilsport, I myself don't see how these patterns can have any effect on us. But there is one pattern up there that *is* important. If you live in the country, far from the glare of street lights, and you pick a really dark, Moonless night, you should be able to see a broad band of faint light stretching overhead from one horizon to the other. It is called the Milky Way.

The Milky Way

My mother taught me that every night a procession of junks carrying lanterns moves silently across the sky, and the water sprinkled from their paddles falls to the earth in the form of dew. I no longer believe that the stars are junks carrying lanterns, no longer that the dew is shaken from their oars.

Allen Upward

The stars are gathered together in a great flat disc called the Milky Way Galaxy. Our star (the Sun) is placed about two thirds of the way out from the centre of the disc. When we look up at the Milky Way in the sky, we are looking *along* the disc towards its centre. That's where most of the stars are to be found, and why they show up as a band of light. Look away from the Milky Way, and we look *out* of the disc, where there are not so many stars.

The stars of the Galaxy do not sit still in space. They slowly rotate around the centre of the disc. What keeps them on their course? The gravity pull of the other stars and stuff that makes up the Galaxy – the same kind of gravity that holds the Earth on course around the Sun, and the Moon around the Earth, and keeps you and me from drifting off into space.

Ring-mistress of the circus of the stars,
Their prancing carousels, their ferris wheels
Lit brilliant in celebration. Thanks to her
All's gala in the galaxy.

                Down here she
Walks us just right, not like the jokey moon
Burlesquing our human stride to kangaroo hops;
Not like vast planets, whose unbearable mass
Would crush us in a bear hug to their surface
And into the surface, flattened. No: deals fairly.
Makes happy each with each: the willow bend
Just so, the acrobat land true, the keystone
Nestle in place for bridge and for cathedral.
Lets us pick up – or mostly – what we need:
Rake, bucket, stone to build with, logs for warmth,
The fallen fruit, the fallen child . . . ourselves.

from 'Gravity' – *J. F. N. Klutz*

47

The Sun (and its planets) takes 200 million years to complete each turn around the centre of the Galaxy – another of the rhythms of space.

Our Milky Way Galaxy is not the only collection of stars. There are many other galaxies. The same swirling pattern of stars repeats itself as far away as our telescopes can see.

When the Fires Go Out

Stars cannot keep shining for ever. Like any other fire, in the end they burn up all their fuel. You might think that means the star would slowly cool down and quietly fizzle out like a bonfire. Not so.

Take the Sun, for example. It has a nasty surprise in store for us.

Ode on a Distant Prospect of Eton College

Alas, regardless of their doom,
The little victims play!
No sense have they of ills to come,
Nor care beyond today.

Thomas Gray

When it starts to run low on fuel, the Sun will gradually swell up to become much bigger than it is now. It will swallow up planet Mercury and possibly Venus as well. It is not expected to reach as far as the Earth. No matter. The surface of the Earth will become bakingly hot. All life will be burned up. (But *not* to worry. None of this is due to happen for another 5,000 million years. I don't want you getting nightmares.)

When a star swells up like this, we say it has become a *red giant* – because of its colour and size. After that, it shrinks down small and becomes white hot; it is then a *white dwarf*. Finally, at long last, it fizzles out.

> A giant sun fills up half the sky in lurid glare;
> the air is gone, the seas are dry,
> the Earth is fused glass, bare.
> The sun becomes a globe immense,
> day, night, are done,
> expanded, massive, glowing, thence
> Earth's orbit is outrun.
>
> If now the outcome is foretold –
> the giant red sun
> collapses, fire-exhausted, cold,
> its evolution run,
> reduced into a faint white dwarf,
> and thence decreasing,
> a dead and light-extinguished dwarf
> with all reaction ceasing.
>
> from 'The End of the World' – *Paul Dignan*

In ancient times, when a king died, his wives were also put to death by burning – so that they could continue to be with him in death. In much the same way, the Sun, when it finally dies, will be attended by the charred remains of its faithful companion, the Earth. Together they face a future of freezing cold – one destined to last for ever.

Fire and Ice

Some say the world will end in fire,
Some say in ice.
From what I've tasted of desire
I hold with those who favor fire.
But if it had to perish twice,
I think I know enough of hate
To say that for destruction ice
Is also great
And would suffice.

Robert Frost

Where Did We Come From?

I have described how stars like the Sun end their lives. But how did they get started in the first place?

To begin with, the Universe was full of gases. That's all – just wind blowing about. All the other stuff – like dirt and metals and the materials that make up our bodies – didn't appear until later.

What happened was that gravity gathered the gases together and squashed them down into balls. As these got tighter and tighter, they heated up (much like air squashed in a bicycle pump gets warm). In fact, some balls of gas got so hot, they caught fire. That's how the first stars were born. Being so hot, some of the particles of gas stuck together to form bigger, heavier particles – the kind that were later to make rocks, and metals, and you and me. This took millions of years.

When I Was the Wind

When I was the wind
I travelled
all the time
now that
I'm a rock
I have a lot
of time
inside of me

Zaro Weil

But the trouble is you can't make people and things in the middle of a white-hot star – obviously. Somehow the newly made stuff – the ashes of the stellar fires – had to be got out. But how? Luckily for us, there was a way. When really big stars get old, they don't just gently swell up to become red giants. They go out with a bang. It's like a gigantic bomb going off. It's called a *supernova explosion*. The explosion throws out some of the ashes. These are later gathered together (by gravity once more) to make new stars – like the Sun, and for the first time, rocky planets. Such planets were not possible earlier because until now there had been no dust or dirt floating around. And that's how the Earth was formed.

The Earth was at just the right distance from the Sun to allow life in all its many forms to evolve out of the dust and mud on its surface. The first to appear were very simple creatures like bugs and bacteria; then more interesting creatures like little fishes and reptiles came along; next, ape-like beings; and from them, human beings finally evolved.

Evolution

Out of the dust a shadow;
Then, a spark;
Out of the cloud a silence,
Then, a lark;
Out of the heart a rapture,
Then, a pain;
Out of the dead, cold ashes,
Life Again.

John Banister Tabb

It is quite a thought that everything we see around us today was once up there in the heavens, being made in a star over a time measured in millions of years.

> To see a World in a Grain of Sand
> And a Heaven in a Wild Flower,
> Hold Infinity in the palm of your hand
> And Eternity in an hour.

> from 'Auguries of Innocence' – *William Blake*

And that goes for ourselves. Our very own bodies are made from stardust.

Identity

> If there is no moon tonight,
> after supper let us sit
> at the window and gaze out
> towards the far sky;
> with no moonlight to
> overwhelm our eyes,
> we will be able to see
> into the night . . . and throw
> our deepest thoughts
> to the singing stars;
> their light is gentle,
> soothing to the soul . . .
> how many dreams dance in the
> Milky Way, to the rhapsody
> played by the cosmic orchestra?
> Peace . . . pouring down upon
> the Earth from space . . .

How many stars stir in the dark,
striking a beam of light
across the ocean which
divides them from us?
Are we not like them?
Is there not, in each of us,
a burning flame . . . sometimes
concentrated . . . other times
diffused?
Do we not have within us
every elemental particle
of the universe?
Are we not then the children
of the stars?

If there is no moon tonight,
after supper let us sit
at the window and gaze out,
towards the far sky . . .

Patti Lynn

Debris in Space

The light from a star twinkles because it is having to pass through the Earth's atmosphere. The atmosphere is always moving about, deflecting the starlight, first one way, then another. That's why the star's brightness seems to change. The changes happen any old how; there's no pattern to them. That's because there is no regular pattern to the movements of the air.

Imagine the astronomers' surprise then when they discovered a star for which the brightness changed in an absolutely regular way: bright . . . dim . . . bright . . . dim . . . bright . . . dim . . . It was as regular as a clock. Because of the regular pulses, it was called a *pulsar*. But what was it? Were these signals from some space aliens trying to make contact with us?

Pulsars in Poetry

Twinkle, twinkle, pulsing star
Newest puzzle from afar.
Beeping on and on you sing –
Are you saying anything?
Twinkle, twinkle more, pulsar,
How I wonder what you are.

Jay M. Pasachoff

No, it wasn't space aliens. The pulsar was found to be at the very place where a supernova explosion had once occurred. Remember, I said that such explosions threw out *some* of the material of the star. You might have wondered what happened to the rest. Well, we now know that the core of the old star collapses down under the weight of its own gravity to form a very small ball. The star starts off big enough to hold a million Earths, but ends up as a tightly packed ball just a few kilometres across.

And it spins. You know how an ice-skater can be spinning quite slowly at first with her arms stretched out wide. But then she makes herself smaller by pulling her arms in to her sides, and that makes her spin so fast she becomes a blur. That is how it is with stars. They start out big and slowly spinning. But when they are squashed down to pulsar size, the spin speeds up. The pulsar sends out a beam of radio-type waves, and the spin whirls this beam around like a beam from a lighthouse. And that's what we pick up here on Earth – the regular pulse of that 'lighthouse beam' as it sweeps past our position.

A pulsar is one kind of debris left over after a supernova explosion. But it is not the only one. The other is even more interesting – and frightening. It's called a *black hole*.

Black Hole

Help me, Lord, I'm
slipping through.
Help me, Lord, I'm
falling.

I'm being pulled in
to a dense black hole
from which there's
no returning.

It's yawning wide;
it's sucking me in,
but there's nothing to see,
it's as black as sin.

Help me, Lord, I'm
sinking down.
Help me,
Lord,
I'm
drowning . . .

Adrian Rumble

Black holes are formed when really, really heavy stars collapse down after they have exploded. Because they are *so* heavy, their gravity is powerful enough that nothing can resist it. The star collapses down to pulsar size, but then carries on, and on, and on, until it ends up with no size at all! It is even smaller than a full stop. And that dot of a star is surrounded by such a powerful gravity force that anything coming too close to it gets sucked in – even light itself. And once inside, there is no escape – you are squashed out of existence. Ugh!

Ah but, you might be thinking, if black holes only suck in light and don't give any out, how can we ever see them? How do we know they are there?

The Wind

Who has seen the wind?
Neither I nor you;
But when the leaves hang trembling
The wind is passing through.

Who has seen the wind?
Neither you nor I;
But when the trees bow down their heads
The wind is passing by.

Christina Rossetti

That's the clue. We may not be able to see the black hole itself, but we can watch what it does to other things that we *can* see. Just as the invisible wind gives itself away by making the leaves move, so we can detect the presence of a black hole by watching what it does to nearby clouds of gas and dust. What we see is that the clouds get caught up and swirl about, and finally get sucked into one particular point in space – rather like water being swirled around the bath before being sucked down the plug hole and out of sight. When we see the behaviour of those clouds, we know *something* must be swallowing them up – that something being the black hole.

Back to the Very Beginning

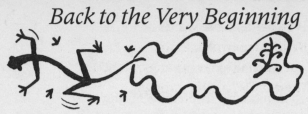

It takes time for light to reach us from a distant star. Light travels very fast (300,000 kilometres per second). But even at that speed, the distances to the stars are so immense that, by the time the light gets here, for all we know, the original star might no longer exist – it could have exploded a long time ago. So, when we look through the telescope, we are not only looking far out into space, we are also looking back in time – how the Universe was *then*, rather than how it is *now*. A funny thought that, don't you think?

Stars

They present light as evidence of the past;
Their brightness reaches us from another time:
They were there when the earth was waste,
When life slithered out of humid slime.

They were there to keep concepts in sight,
To hold a pattern as a path above
The darkness, to be the guiding light
When men walked upright, saw them, fell in love.

Alan Bold

Looking back in time makes us wonder how the Universe began. It began with a great explosion: the *Big Bang*.

61

Galactic Diary of an Edwardian Lady

In the beginning was a black bomb
That blew apart. A blinding smoke
Kept growing, growing

To a tropical fog, intolerably bright.
From this, white whorls of moonshine mist
Distilled, and then distilled

To petal-eddies on a dark pool.
And now they spin in clusters
Farther and farther apart

Like shining catkins, twisted into spools.
All forms, all time, all complexity,
From the first snowdrop to muffins and tea

Lay in that round black bomb
And will return there
When the hot afternoon is done.

Edward Larrissy

Out of the Big Bang there came only the lightest gases; anything heavier would have been smashed to bits by all the heat and violence. The gases later collected together to form galaxies of stars – as you already know by now.

The Big Bang happened 12,000 million years ago. It saw the creation of everything in the Universe. Not only that, it marked the creation of time – the start of time itself. There was no time before the Big Bang; there was no 'before'.

Time

Who made time?
Was it God?
Yes! He made all things.
When did he make time?
Yes. When?

He created time at the beginning.
At the beginning of what?
At the beginning of time.
When was that?
Yes. When?

That was before time began.
What was there before?
Nothing, absolutely nothing.
Since when was there nothing?
Yes. Since when?

It was there all the time.

R. F. Enever, a pupil from Pimlico, London

As time carries on, old stars die, while new ones are born.

The Unending Sky

I could not sleep for thinking of the sky,
The unending sky, with all its million suns
Which turn their planets everlastingly
In nothing, where the fire-haired comet runs.
If I could sail that nothing, I should cross
Silence and emptiness with dark stars passing;
Then, in the darkness, see a point of gloss
Burn to a glow, and glare, and keep massing,
And rage into a sun with wandering planets,
And drop behind; and then, as I proceed,
See his last light upon his last moon's granites
Die to a dark that would be night indeed:
Night where my soul might sail a million years
In nothing, not even Death, not even tears.

John Masefield

And What of the Future?

We have learned how the Universe began. How will it end?

When we look through our telescopes at the distant galaxies, we see that they are all receding from us – they are flying off into the distance. The further away a galaxy is, the faster it is receding into the distance. This is all because of the Big Bang. Everything is still flying apart after the explosion. So, will this carry on for ever?

Although the galaxies are moving apart, we expect them to be slowing down. This is because all the galaxies are pulling on each other with their gravity forces. Gravity is trying desperately to hold on to them and stop them from getting away.

If gravity is strong enough, it will one day bring all the galaxies to a halt. From then on, they will start to come together once more. They speed up. The sky brightens and becomes blindingly bright. In the end, all the stars come crashing in on top of each other, all at the same moment – *The Big Crunch*.

The Expanding Universe

The furthest stars recede
Faster than the earth itself to our need.
For far beyond the furthest, where

Light is snatched backward, no
Star leaves echo or shadow
To prove it has ever been there.
And if the universe
Reversed and showed
The colour of its money;
If now unobservable light
Flowed inward, and the skies snowed
A blizzard of galaxies,
The lens of night would burn
Brighter than the focussed sun,
And man turn blinded
With white-hot darkness in his eyes.

Norman Nicholson

That is one way the Universe might end. But these days, we reckon the end will be very different.

We think that gravity is not strong enough to pull everything back together in a Big Crunch. It might be strong enough to slow everything down to walking pace in the infinite future, but not to bring it all back.

If that is the case, then we look to a future where eventually all the stars burn out. No more stars form. Everything becomes cold and lifeless – not just here on Earth, but everywhere in the Universe. This we call the *Heat Death of the Universe*.

Cosmic Death

By death the moon was gathered in
Long ago, ah long ago;
Yet still the silver corpse must spin
And with another's light must glow.
Her frozen mountains must forget
Their primal hot volcanic breath,
Doomed to revolve for ages yet,
Void amphitheatres of death.

And all about the cosmic sky,
The black that lies beyond our blue,
Dead stars innumerable lie,
And stars of red and angry hue
Not dead but doomed to die.

Julian Huxley

Which all sounds pretty grim and depressing, don't you think?

Not really. At least, that's not how *I* see it. The Universe is a home for life – for you and me. Just think of how many billions upon billions of people will have lived their lives before the Heat Death comes – not to mention the zillions upon zillions of space aliens that might be out there on other planets going around other suns. That is surely enough life for anyone. I reckon the Universe, having put up with us lot for so long, will by then deserve a good long rest.

Space Travel

The story I have told so far has depended on what we have been able to see through our telescopes. We have been viewing distant, far-off places. It has been a bit like leafing through those glossy booklets you pick up from travel agents. But looking at pictures of exotic foreign lands is not the same as actually visiting them.

I told you earlier about a visit I made to the cinema when I was a boy. I used to go regularly on Saturday mornings. My hero in those days was Flash Gordon. Each Saturday we would thrill to another episode of his space adventures. Like most children at the time, I used to dream of one day going on an exciting visit to the planets. (Recently I saw one of those old Flash Gordon films. I couldn't believe how truly *awful* it was!)

Shed in Space

My Grandad Lewis
On my mother's side
Had two ambitions.
One was to take first prize
For shallots at the village show
And the second
Was to be a space commander.

Every Tuesday
After I'd got their messages,
He'd lead me with a wink
To his garden shed
And there, amongst the linseed
And the sacks of peat and horse manure
He'd light his pipe
And settle in his deck chair.
His old eyes on the blue and distant
That no one else could see,
He'd ask,
'Are we A OK for lift off?'
Gripping the handles of the lawn mower
I'd reply:
'A OK'
And then
Facing the workbench,
In front of shelves of paint and creosote
And racks of glistening chisels
He'd talk to Mission Control.
'Five-Four-Three-Two-One-Zero –
We have lift off.'
This is Grandad Lewis talking,
'Do you read me?
Britain's first space shed
Is rising majestically into orbit
From its launch pad
In the allotments
In Lakey Lane.'
And so we'd fly,

Through timeless afternoons
Till tea time came,
Amongst the planets
And mysterious suns,
While the world
Receded like a dream:
Grandad never won
That prize for shallots,
But as the captain
Of an intergalactic shed
There was no one to touch him.

Gareth Owen

Eventually space travel became a reality. The first rocket lifted off.

Space Shot

Out of the furnace
The great fish rose
Its silver tail on fire
But with a slowness
Like something sorry
To be rid of earth.
The boiling mountains
Of snow white cloud
Searched for a space to go into
And the ground thundered
With a roar
That set tea cups
Rattling in a kitchen
Twenty miles away.
Across the blue it arched
Milk bottle white
But shimmering in the haze.
And the watchers by the fence
Held tinted glass against their eyes
And wondered at what man could do
To make so large a thing
To fly so far and free.
While the unknown Universe waited;
For waiting
Was what it had always been good at.

Gareth Owen

At the start it was thought too risky to send up a man or a woman. Going up was not difficult; the worry was whether living things could survive floating around in space for a long time. Besides, there was the problem of how to bring them back to Earth safely. So the first living thing to be sent into space was a dog – a Russian dog called Laika.

Laika showed that we could indeed live in space all right. But after a few days, she had used up all the air in her sputnik craft, and died. The craft and her body were burned up as they crashed back into the atmosphere once more.

Animals are used in experiments when it is too dangerous for humans – for example when trying out new medicines. Yes, it's sad when this has to happen. But scientists try not to use them any more than is necessary.

Dog in Space

The barking in space
has died out now,
though dogbones rattle.
And the marks of teeth
on the sputnik's hull
are proof of a battle
impossible to win.

And asteroid-dents
were no help at all.
Did the dog see,
through the window,
earth's blue ball?

Did the dog know
that no other dog
had made that circle
around the earth –
her historic spin
that turned eternal?

Matthew Sweeney

When it was the turn for humans to go into space, they couldn't get over how beautiful and inviting the Earth looked from space – all blue and wrapped in fluffy white clouds. It was the first time anyone had been able to see it all – a great ball floating in the black emptiness of space.

Earth

As the glow of the boosters
Floods the sky
The world
Falls away beneath me
Soon the earth cries out
'Come home'
I then felt like a piece of iron
And my home the magnet
The heavens swarm with blackness
Like billions of flies
Looking back
My planet
Seems like a huge glowing emerald
In black diamond-studded dress

The swirling clouds
Wash from a liner
She was an oasis
In the middle of a black desert.

Daniel Batley, aged 11 years

You will have seen the pictures on TV of astronauts floating about weightless in their space craft. You might think this is because there is no gravity up there. But that's not right. The Earth's gravity stretches right out into space. It is the Earth's gravity that is holding the space craft, and the astronaut, in orbit round the Earth. But that's how it all gets 'used up' – stopping them from flying off into outer space; there's none left over to pull the astronaut, or anything else, down onto the floor of the space craft. That's why they all float. And boy, does that cause problems!

In Outer Space

Astronauts in outer space
Don't eat the same as us.
If they had fish and chips and peas
It would cause no end of fuss.
The chips and peas would float around
In weightless jamboree –
And astronauts would all need nets
with which to catch their tea.

Mark Burgess

Then at long last, after many years of dreaming about space travel, humans first set foot on the Moon. It was a proud moment as we watched it happen on TV.

A Giant Leap for Mankind

In fire it came.
In roaring thunder it came,
Ravaging the rocks with a raging hot wind:

A dragon descending in fire and smoke,
Blasting the ground in gritty billows
Of burning dust: dropping like a spider
To settle in smoke and straddle the ground:
A great, steel spider on skeletal legs,
Standing silver, the blackness behind it
As silent now it stood against the sky.
Fearfully we watched:
Hiding we watched and waited
While the dreadful creature crouched in the dust.
And surely our fear was well founded;
For a hole opened high, and a weird white figure
Stood in the space above the plain:
A stocky figure on two feet.
It stooped to push out some projection –
Steps, down which it slid, to stand.
It waved two limbs above its head –
A square head, a faceless head,
Its front a square, polished and reflecting.
The faceless figure as we watched
Stepped and leapt, it seems for nothing.
It carried a pack or burden on its back
But did not seek to set it down.
It leapt about mightily: plainly mad.
We were glad to stay concealed
Till the monster remounted its terrible tower.

Why should this come to shake our world
Just to cavort, we wondered?

Richard Tysoe

Over De Moon

Dere's a man on de moon
He's skipping an stuff,
Dere's a man on de moon
He looks very tuff,
Dere's a man on de moon
An he's all alone,
Dere's a man on de moon
His wife is at home.

He's dancing around
To real moony music,
He carries his air
He knows how to use it,
He waves to his wife
Still on Planet E,
She's waving back
But he cannot see.

De man on de moon is so clever,
He has sum ideas to persue,
His chewing gum can last fe ever
His fast food is already chewed.

Dere's a man on de moon
He has a spaceship,
Dere's a man on de moon
An we payed fe it,

Dere's a man on de moon
His mission ain't done,
Dere's a man on de moon
He's after de Sun.

Benjamin Zephaniah

Since then we have sent unmanned space craft to the other
planets. They have landed on Mars, and flown past others to
give us close-up pictures. There is much more exploration to
be done of the Solar System.

And after that? The trouble is that beyond our furthest planet Pluto, there lie vast expanses of space before one reaches even the nearest star.

End of the Road in Space

'We're here?'
'Where?'
'You know.'
'No.'
'On a . . . in a . . . place.'
'But . . . this is a nowhere place.'
'This is the nowhere they call space.'

Michael Rosen

Any astronaut setting out on a journey to a star will have died of old age long before the craft reaches its destination.

No, the possibilities of space travel seem limited. Which perhaps means we would be better off learning how to look after our own planet – how to care for each other.

Song in Space

When man first flew beyond the sky
He looked back into the world's blue eye.
Man said: What makes your eye so blue?
Earth said: The tears in the ocean do.
Why are the seas so full of tears?
Because I've wept so many thousand years.
Why do you weep as you dance through space?
Because I am the Mother of the Human Race.

Adrian Mitchell

The more we have learned about space and what exists out there, the more it makes us realize just what a wonderful, friendly place our own Earth is.

The World

Great, wide, beautiful, wonderful World,
With the wonderful water round you curled,
And the wonderful grass upon your breast –
World, you are beautifully drest.

The wonderful air is over me,
And the wonderful wind is shaking the tree,
It walks on the water, and whirls the mills,
And talks to itself on the tops of the hills.

You friendly Earth, how far do you go,
With the wheatfields that nod and the rivers that flow,
With cities and gardens, and cliffs, and isles,
And people upon you for thousands of miles?

Ah, you are so great, and I am so small,
I tremble to think of you, World, at all;
And yet, when I said my prayers today,
A whisper inside me seemed to say,
'You are more than the Earth, though you are such a dot:
You can love and think, and the Earth cannot.

William Brighty Rands

One More Thing

I hope you have enjoyed this look at the Universe. As I said at the very start, I find it all quite fascinating and mind-boggling.

But I can also well imagine that it has left you feeling a little uneasy. When we think of how big everything is out there – the planets, the stars, the galaxies, and space itself – it is natural for us to feel small and unimportant ourselves.

Small, yes; we certainly are small compared to heavenly bodies like the Earth, Sun, and stars. But that does not mean we are less important. Why do I say that? Because we have *minds* – minds that are able to think about the Earth, Sun, and stars. They, on the other hand, do not think about us. This is not because we are not worth thinking about; it is because *they* can't think about *anything*.

Let me ask you a question: Which would you rather be: the Earth, the Sun, a star – or *yourself*? The answer is pretty obvious, isn't it. As the final words of that last poem put it . . .

'You are more than the Earth, though you are such a dot:
You can love and think, and the Earth cannot.'

Acknowledgements

MARK BURGESS: 'In Outer Space' from *Feeling Peckish* (Methuen), by permission of Egmont Children's Books Limited. GILLIAN CLARKE: 'Eclipse of the Moon' from *Selected Poems*, by permission of Carcanet Press Limited. WALTER DE LA MARE: 'The Magnifying Glass' from *The Complete Poems of Walter de la Mare* (Faber and Faber, 1969), by permission of the Literary Trustees of Walter de la Mare, and the Society of Authors as their representative. ELEANOR FARJEON: 'The Meteors' from *Then There were Three* (Michael Joseph), by permission of David Higham Associates Limited. ROBERT FROST: 'Fire and Ice' from *The Poetry of Robert Frost*, edited by Edward Connery Latham (Jonathan Cape), to the Estate of Robert Frost and Random House UK Ltd. A. E. HOUSMAN: 'Stars, I have Seen them Fall', by permission of the Society of Authors as the Literary Representative of the Estate of A. E. Housman. TED HUGHES: 'The Harvest Moon' from *New Selected Poems 1957–1994* (Faber and Faber 1995), by permission of Faber and Faber Ltd. JOHN MASEFIELD: 'The Unending Sky', by permission of the Society of Authors as the Literary Representative of the Estate of John Masefield. ROGER MCGOUGH: 'Shooting Stars' from *Lucky* (Viking Penguin), reprinted by permission of the Peters Fraser and Dunlop Group Limited on behalf of Roger McGough. WES MAGEE: 'How to Reach the Sun . . . on a Piece of Paper' from *Sandwich Poets: Matt, Wes and Pete* (Macmillan, 1995), by kind permission of the author. SPIKE MILLIGAN: 'Rain', by kind permission of Spike Milligan Productions Ltd. ADRIAN MITCHELL: 'Song in Space' from *Balloon Lagoon and the Magic Islands* (Orchard, 1977), reprinted by permission of the Peters Fraser and Dunlop Group Limited on behalf of Adrian Mitchell. NORMAN NICHOLSON: 'The Expanding Universe' from *Collected Poems* (Faber and Faber, 1994), by permission of Faber and Faber Ltd. KATHLEEN RAINE: 'The World' from *Collected Poems* (HarperCollins), by permission of HarperCollins Publishers. MICHAEL ROSEN: 'End of the Road in Space', to the Peters, Fraser & Dunlop Group Limited on behalf of the author. MATTHEW SWEENEY: 'Splat' and 'Dog in Space' from *Fatso in the Red Suit* (Faber and Faber, 1995), by permissions of Faber and Faber Ltd. STEVE TURNER: 'Sun' from *The Day I Fell Down the Toilet*, published in 1996 by Lion Publishing plc, reproduced by permission. ZARO WEIL: 'When I was the Wind' from *Mud Moon and Me*, first published in the UK in 1989 by Orchard Books, a division of the Watts Publishing Group, 96 Leonard Street, London, EC2A 4RH. BENJAMIN ZEPHANIAH: 'Over De Moon' from *Talking Turkeys* (Viking Penguin), by permission of Penguin UK

Faber and Faber Ltd apologize for any errors or omissions in the above list and would be grateful to be notified of any corrections that should be incorporated in the next edition of this volume.